"TRUE" REFLECTIONS IN A MIRROR

by

Carolyn J. Pitarra

RoseDog Books
PITTSBURGH, PENNSYLVANIA 15222

This book is a fiction. The characters used are fictitious, imaginative and bear no semblance to existing persons. Some of the towns used are not in the exact setting.

RoseDog Books
701 Smithfield Street
Pittsburgh, PA 15222
Visit our website at *www.rosedogbookstore.com*

ISBN: 978-1-4349-8944-4
eISBN: 978-1-4349-7936-0

IN

MEMORY

OF

JODY

- 1 -

Carmela's Coffee Shoppe was bustling with activity and very overcrowded that extremely wet Friday morning when Valerie arrived. People passing by had simply dashed in to escape the violent thunderstorm typical of Boston during the spring and she was fortunate to get the last available seat at the far end of the counter. From where Valerie sat, she was able to see through the fogged up windows the building across the street where the C & J Publishing Company was located. The huge digital clock over the door revealed she still had plenty of time to review her manuscript before her impending appointment with Gordon Richardson. Motioning to the busy waiter to pour her a second cup of coffee, and reaching into her pocketbook for a pencil, she began to read and edit the words which had become so familiar to her. Unfortunately whenever Valerie was writing she would become so completely absorbed in her thoughts and ideas that she would always lose track of the time. Jumping down from her stool and quickly gathering up the scattered pages of her book from the counter, she managed to elbow her way through the crowd hoping that she would not be late for her scheduled appointment.

Valerie was anxiously scraping the mud from her precious manuscript when the elevator light blinked '42nd' Floor. 'I hope that taxi driver gets a ticket,' she thought to herself as her mind glanced back to the scene moments earlier. A taxi speeding through the rain soaked streets of Boston had thoroughly drenched her while she was hurriedly crossing the street from the coffee shoppe where she had spent most of the morning editing her now soggy and very wrinkled manuscript. It had taken Val almost three years to arrange a meeting with the owner of the C & J Publishing Company and she was not about to let a rude taxi driver and a little water ruin the chances of getting her manuscript published. She had worked too hard and had given up too much.

As she softy knocked on Gordon Richardson's door, the rain water dripping from her new and very expensive suit did not concern her as much as the butterflies she now felt fluttering in the pit of her stomach. A rough, rasping voice from behind the door muttered, "Yeah, it's open."

Val took a deep breath and cautiously stepped into the biggest office she had ever been in, and even bigger was the figure sitting behind the desk. "Ex....excuse me, Mr. Richardson," Val stammered as she slowly approached his desk.

"Thank you for allowing me this time with you. My name is Val....Valerie Ficarro. I was hoping you would be able to read over my manuscript in your spare time of course and advise me if it is something you would consider publishing."

Valerie knew she was speaking way too fast and a bit too loudly.

"This is my first attempt at writing a book and you are the only publisher who has agreed to personally meet with me and I would appreciate any guidance and assistance you can provide. It has taken me over two years to write my novel and I am hoping to finally have it published."

Gordon Richardson sat mindlessly drumming his fingers on the top of his mahogany desk and watched intently as Valerie walked towards him. His eyes were completely focused on her long, well-curved legs, that he barely noticed the water still dripping from her herring-bone suit onto his newly installed, plush blue carpet. He had been in the publishing business for many years and could still appreciate the freshness and beauty of a young wanna-be author. He had seen hundreds of them come and go and this one was no different. Maybe prettier.

"Okay, I'll look it over," he offered half-heartily, but it will take me a while before I can get to it."

Reaching down and sliding open the bottom drawer of his desk, he carelessly tossed in her manuscript. Valerie was able to get a glimpse of the stack of papers that were stuffed in the drawer and her heart began to languish as she realized there were hundreds of other writers who had also approached Mr. Richardson with their manuscripts. Turning to leave, she managed to whisper a polite 'thank you' and made a silent promise to herself to remain hopeful in spite of his apparent coolness and obvious lack of interest.

What Valerie had no way of knowing at the time was that Mr. Richardson had his own problems to deal with and reading manuscripts was not one of them. His life was falling apart and it was getting worse with each passing day. He had recently found out that his wife, Claire, was having an affair with an acquaintance of his and that Luke, his teenage son, had been caught smoking pot at school. The only "normal" family member was his musically-gifted daughter, Jill, who was giving a piano recital that very afternoon. He was hoping to catch her performance and, as soon as that young woman left his office, he immediately began to clear off his desk. It took him only a few minutes to finish and as he stood up to grab his coat from the rack, he could hear an alarm screeching loudly from the corridor.

'Another prank,' he thought to himself. Once a month someone always manages to set off that damn fire alarm.' But when Gordon opened the door to his office, the screams and commotion radiating throughout the hallway told him that this was not a prank. Something very serious was wrong. "What happened?" he shouted to a few people who were quickly running past him with looks of horror on their faces. He reached out and grabbed a woman's arm as gently as he could and demanded that she tell him what was going on.

"It's the elevator!" she yelled, while pointing to the main elevator across the hall from his office. "Something went terribly wrong and it has crashed to the floor below. Leave the building while you still can. Take the stairs!"

The young woman who had just left his office immediately came to his mind and he wondered if she was one of the occupants on that doomed elevator. 'What was her name,' he kept asking himself over and over, as if by doing so he would be able to recall it. 'Vera....Vivian...something like that,' but he just could not remember. He quickly turned to take the stairway leading to the street below and silently hoped that she had done the same. The heavy rain had tapered off to a slight drizzle by the time Gordon exited the building and ambulances, fire trucks, and a crowd of spectators were starting to assemble. He noticed Ralph Thomas, the owner of the building, talking with a police officer and motioned him over.

"Ralph, what the hell happened? Wasn't that elevator supposed to be refurbished months ago?"

"Yeah, evidently my damn janitor forgot to tighten and grease the cables and one of them severed. Do you know if any of your employees were on it?" Ralph asked in a shaky voice.

"Fortunately none of them were as I gave them the day off. They have been working a lot of overtime for me lately and deserved a long weekend. Do you know yet if there are any casualties?" asked Gordon in a concerned voice.

Ralph began to scratch the top of his head, which was his habit whenever he was asked a question that made him uncomfortable.

"I'm not sure yet, but I think there are a few who may have sustained life-threatening injuries."

"That's terrible," replied Gordon shaking his head. "It's a good thing today is Friday or there might have been a lot more people on that elevator. I'm sorry I can't stick around due to a family commitment, but be sure to give me a call later if there is anything I can do to help. And by the way, I'd fire that janitor if I were you."

"Thanks," answered Ralph. "I certainly appreciate your offer, but it looks like I will have to replace that elevator with a brand new one. I also better get myself a good lawyer as I have a sneaky feeling that it won't be long before I'm involved in a huge lawsuit. Christ, that's all I need."

The two men shook hands and as Gordon continued on his way he couldn't help but think that money always seemed to matter more to Ralph than people did.

- 2 -

The piano studio where his daughter Jill had been taking lessons for almost three years was only a couple of blocks from his office, so he decided to walk as he could definitely use the exercise. Gordon had already started to gain the extra pounds associated with middle-age, and eating out on a regular basis certainly didn't help his slowly expanding waistline. As he walked, he thought about Claire and wondered if she would also be at their daughter's recital, or was she too busy with her own plans to even remember.

Gordon and Claire were married at a young age and had enjoyed many years together while raising their two children. His career in the publishing business was very successful and he now owned his own company, the C & J Publishing Company, named after his wife and daughter. Claire was a stay-at-home mother who was extremely involved in social issues and had volunteered numerous times at various community events throughout the city.

Gordon was not exactly sure when they had started to drift apart but as the years passed, he knew they were spending less and less time together, each involved in their own dreams while living disconnected lives. He blamed himself for the distance that had come between them as his job was very demanding and he often spent more time at the office than he did at home.

Eventually they agreed to remain together until the children were out of school and living on their own before going their separate ways.

Agreements, however, can be broken, and it wasn't long before Claire became romantically involved with Gordon's long-time friend, Dr. Evan May. He and Evan had been college roommates and even in those days Evan had a keen eye for the girls on campus, usually dating two or three simultaneously. They had lost touch after graduating from college until a few years ago when they reconnected at a local eye clinic. Gordon was having a problem with his eyesight and needed to see a specialist, so Claire had scheduled him an appointment with Dr. May, who as luck would have it turned out to be his old friend from college. Perhaps it was not luck after all, as a short time later Evan and Claire began seeing each other and it was not just at the eye clinic.

- 3 -

Gordon could hear the soft music flowing from the open window of the piano studio while he quickly took the stairs two at a time. Entering the music room, he could see his beautiful daughter's fingers dancing across the black and white keys creating a rhythm and harmony that even Mozart might enjoy. He was extremely proud of Jill and as he sat listening to her play, he wondered from whom she had inherited her extraordinary musical ability. He knew it was definitely not from his side of the family and he doubted if it was from Claire's side. Even Jill's teenage brother, Luke, who loved all kinds of music, could only carry a tune while in the shower. Gordon's thoughts were interrupted by the loud applause as Jill stood up to take a bow.

"What was the name of the song you just played?" Gordon asked his daughter while lifting a glass of wine to his lips. Claire had not shown up for Jill's recital, so he invited his daughter to have dinner with him afterwards at a nearby restaurant.

"Jeepers, Dad, that song is one of my favorite pieces that I composed about five months ago and I call it, 'Reflections In A Mirror.' You must have heard me playing it on the piano thousands of times at home."

Gordon jokingly admitted that it did have a slightly familiar ring to it. He told Jill that he enjoyed it immensely and suggested she may want to pursue her music more fervently, perhaps even consider writing a book on the subject which, of course, he would be more than happy to publish for her.

They were almost finished with dessert when Gordon could no longer remain silent about the disaster that happened earlier in his office building. He did not want to ruin Jill's special moment with such shocking news, but he thought it would be better if she heard it from him rather than later on the nightly news broadcast.

"Jill....I need to tell you about something terrible that happened at work today. The janitor of the building neglected to grease the cables on that old Methuselah elevator across the hall from my office and it crashed to the floor below." Jill sat in total silence while her father spoke of the tragedy, not knowing what to say or how to respond. She was just 15 years old and in her short lifespan things like that happened only in the movies.

"Oh, my God, that's insane!!" was her teenage reply. "Dad, that's the elevator you always use! Did you know anyone who was on it?"

"I don't think so." he replied, "There was a pretty, young woman who had just left my office who might have been on it, but I have no way of knowing for sure."

Jill was well aware that her mother and father were having some marital problems so she assumed that this young, pretty woman her father was referring to was probably his girlfriend.

"The names of any victims will be posted in the newspaper tomorrow, so you can check the list for her name. I hope she is okay though," Jill quickly added hoping her father wouldn't think she was glad his girlfriend may have died in that disastrous elevator accident. Taking the last bite of his apple pie, Gordon pushed his chair slightly away from the table and motioned to the waiter for the bill.

"That's the problem," he began. "I don't remember her name. She told me but I just can't remember what she said. Maybe if I see it in print, that will jog my memory." At least he hoped it would.

- 4 -

As usual, the house was completely dark when Gordon pulled into the driveway. He felt very rueful ending a perfect night out with his lovely daughter because it was not often that he got to spend quality time with her. She was always busy and on the go doing things that teenagers do, which included spending time with Scott, her latest boyfriend. Gordon was apprehensive about the relationship as it seemed to be getting a little too serious. Even Claire had noticed and once remarked that she thought Jill and Scott were spending too much time alone together and would he have a talk with her about it. He was thinking perhaps tonight would be the perfect time for that talk, but as he unlocked the kitchen door, he could hear the up stair's phone ringing. Jill darted past him excitedly shouting, "that must be Scott!" and he instinctively knew the father/daughter talk would have to wait.

It was almost time for the 11:00 o'clock news as Gordon mixed himself a scotch and soda and fluffed up the pillow on which he had been dozing. Checking the time, he was surprised that he had been asleep for just a little over an hour. He felt as if he had been sleeping for days and, in anticipation of the upcoming news broadcast, wished that he had been. The loud banging of the garage door slamming shut startled him at first, but then he remembered it must be Claire just getting home from one of her book club meetings. A cynical voice in his mind told him that the meeting most likely had been with Evan or why else would she be getting home at this late hour?

Claire was feeling a little guilty as she opened the hall closet to hang up her coat. Many of her friends, some of whom she had not seen in years, were at the Book Club meeting and they spent hours reviewing not only the books they had just read but also their own lives. Andrea and Elizabeth, two of her best friends, had recently separated from their husbands and Natalie was currently in the middle of getting a nasty divorce. Claire smiled to herself as she thought about the torrid love affair she was having with Evan and for a minute wondered if she should share this news with them or keep it to herself. She decided it might not be a good idea to reveal her lifestyle to her friends at this particular time, but to keep it a secret at least for now. Noticing that it was getting late, she got up from the couch and while buttoning her coat heard Natalie squeal:

"Claire, you can't leave now! We're just starting to have fun!"

She quickly made up the excuse that her son, Luke, was at a friend's house and that she had promised to pick him up at a certain time.

'I wonder what they would think of me,' she thought, 'if they knew I was really meeting my lover at a local motel? They probably wouldn't believe it.'

Claire had a hard time believing it herself. She never thought it would be possible for her to fall in love with another man, especially a man like Evan May. When she first met him at the eye clinic, he seemed very arrogant and self-centered, the type of man who could not make a commitment, especially to just one woman. When she had gone back to his office to pick up her husband's new glasses, he had invited her to join him for a drink and in spite of her initial judgment about him, Claire accepted. She assumed there would be no harm in having an innocent drink with Gordon's old college friend, never realizing that it would eventually turn into many drinks that were not so innocent. As she drove into the familiar motel parking lot, her guilty conscience started to surface, and she began to wonder where this was all going and how it would all end. These thoughts quickly evaporated, however, when she saw Evan leaning against his Mercedes with a profuse grin covering his face and clutching an enormous bouquet of daffodils, her favorite flowers.

"Hi sweetheart," said Evan as he pulled her closely to him and kissed her tenderly for a long moment before sweeping her up into his arms.

"I have missed you tremendously these past few weeks that I thought tonight would never get here," he softly whispered in her ear as the door to their special motel room closed tightly behind them.

It was hours later when Claire, smoothing her rumpled skirt while walking into the living room, nodded a silent "hello" to her husband as he was turning up the volume on the television.

"There were only two survivors," the news reporter's voice quietly stated as he ended his report.

"What happened?" asked Claire, "another car bomb in Iraq?" Gordon felt like smacking her across the face for asking such a flippant question, but instead replied through clenched teeth:

"No, this news is not about something that happened thousands of miles away. This tragedy happened right where we live....right where I work, and just like the war, it's a nightmare!"

By the sharp tone of his voice, Claire knew that it would not be wise to pursue the conversation any further. She would just have to wait until tomorrow morning to find out what the hell he was actually talking about.

- 5 -

Jill had showered and was almost dressed before she remembered there was no school. It was Saturday. She thought about going back to bed for a few hours, but changed her mind and decided instead to go downstairs and make herself the usual weekend breakfast of pancakes and scrambled eggs. After breakfast she would vacuum her bedroom and finish her other chores before going to the mall in the afternoon and buy something exquisite to wear on her Saturday night date with Scott. They had made plans to double-date with their friends, Sylvia and Tom, and after having dinner at Cafe Vincenzo's, an up-scale restaurant in Boston's Little Italy, they were going to the movies and she wanted to look extra-nice for this very special occasion! She and Scott had been friends for slightly over a year but lately they were becoming much more than just friends. Jill could hear her parents' voices coming from the kitchen as she came downstairs and wondered why they were up so early on a weekend. Maybe they too had forgotten it was a Saturday.

Gordon had spent a long restless night tossing and turning, even getting up twice to have a cigarette and use the bathroom. He was anxious for the night to end and could not wait to read the morning newspaper's account of the elevator accident. Maybe when he saw it in print it would seem real to him and his thoughts would be less scattered. After pouring himself a cup of coffee, he sat down at the kitchen table to read about yesterday's news. He was already drinking his second cup when the alarm clock upstairs went off jolting Claire wide awake from a sound sleep. It was only seven o'clock in the morning and she was tempted to just lay in bed for a while longer dreaming about Evan and how wonderful last night had been, when suddenly she remembered how upset Gordon was about something he heard on the news. Her curiosity forced her to drag herself out of bed and find out what had happened that caused him such distress.

"Good morning," Jill mumbled as she came into the kitchen, completely startling her parents who were totally absorbed in their discussion about the elevator accident. "What are you doing up already?" asked her mother, "especially on the weekend?" Slurping a large glass of orange juice, Jill explained:

"Mom! Remember I have a special date with Scott tonight. I went to bed real early to make sure I got enough sleep. It's called beauty rest and I would never be able to go anywhere if I have those ugly dark circles under my eyes." "Well, I'll be able to drive you and your friends to the restaurant but how will you get home?" asked her mother in a concerned voice. Jill assured her that arrangements had already been made. Scott's father, Tom Applegate, would pick them up after the movies and had promised to take everyone for ice cream before driving them home.

Gordon, who had been listening intently, quickly grasped his wife's implication that apparently she was not going to be home later that evening, and in a slightly sarcastic tone asked, "Oh, another book club meeting again tonight, Claire?"

She shot him a look that revealed he had hit a nerve, but simply walked out of the kitchen without saying a word.

Gordon was glad to be alone with his daughter for a few minutes so he could continue their conversation from yesterday.

"You were right, Jill, the names of the victims from yesterday's elevator accident are listed in the morning paper and the woman who left my office was on it. Her name was Vickie Fachero and she was just 29 years old. If I had only spent some time talking with her .... if I had showed more of an interest ... if I had only detained her for another five minutes, she would still be alive."

Jill immediately recognized that her father was in some way blaming himself for this woman's death.

"Dad it was not your fault! You had nothing to do with it. It was just an accident."

Deep down Gordon knew that his daughter was right. He could not have prevented the elevator from crashing, but he could have prevented that woman from being on it. This thought would haunt him for a long, long time.

- 6 -

The temperature had risen to 67 degrees by noon, which for Boston was quite warm for this time of the year. Gordon was now at home alone. Claire had left a short time ago to drop Jill off at the mall and on her way home was going to stop at the store to pick up a few groceries. After wasting the entire morning away, he decided to do something productive with the unusually nice afternoon and washing his car seemed like a good idea. He was applying the final coat of wax when a police car pulled up in front of the house with his son Luke in the back seat.

'Oh shit! I wonder what that damn kid has done now,' Gordon thought as he wiped the car wax from his hands. Luke was only 13 years old but already had been caught twice before smoking marijuana with his two older friends. Gordon and Claire had tried to keep a tighter rein on him, but because of their own busy schedules and personal problems, Luke was able to do what he wanted most of the time. And most of the time what he wanted to do was skip school, smoke pot, and hang out with his friends. Most of the time, but not this time.

"Good afternoon officer," Gordon said with an uneasy smile as he stared icily at Luke. "My son is usually not escorted home in a police car. I hope it's nothing serious."

The policeman shook Gordon's extended hand as he explained that Luke and his friends had been caught stealing DVD's from Silence & Sounds, a music store in the Buttercup Mall, and that two small bags of marijuana were found hidden in their shoes. Because Luke was underage, he would have to appear in Children's Court at a later date for the drug possession, but hopefully the music store would not press charges as the DVD's had already been recovered and returned.

"Thank you officer," Gordon managed to whisper in a slightly somber and embarrassed tone before the police car drove away. As he marched his son back inside the house, he was silently praying that none of his nosey neighbors had been peaking out of their windows wondering what a police car was doing at the Richardson's house on a Saturday afternoon.

Luke instinctively knew that he was in deep trouble this time and unless he could hopefully lie his way out of it, he would probably be grounded for at least a year.

'If only Rick, his stupid friend, had kept his big mouth shut he would still be enjoying that blunt in the men's room at the mall. But no, he had to spill his guts to the manager. I hope he gets grounded for life.'

These were the thoughts running through Luke's mind as he felt his father tightly grab his arm and spin him around.

"What the hell is wrong with you?" exclaimed Gordon, whose normally pallid face was now the color of crimson. "You're not only smoking pot, but now you are also stealing!! What else are you doing behind my back that I don't know about?"

Luke just stood there staring down at his feet knowing that the less he said the better it would be for him. He would let his father spit and sputter until eventually he would send him upstairs to his room like he always did and tell him to stay there until his mother came home. Gordon shouted out several other unanswered questions before finally ordering Luke to go upstairs to his room and stay there until his mother came home.

Gordon Richardson began to wonder if anything pleasant was ever again going to happen in his life. With the exception of taking his daughter out to dinner, these last two days had been the worst he could remember in a long time. He was anxious for Monday to come so he could return to his office where he always felt comfortable, relaxed, and in control. Would the tragedy that happened on Friday change all that? He could not be certain, but he felt that the path of his life's journey was about to change and whatever direction it went in, he was definitely looking forward to it.

- 7 -

"Good morning, Mr. Richardson," were the first words Gordon heard as he hesitatingly stepped into the brand new elevator. The installation men had been working diligently all weekend in order to have the new elevator up and running by Monday morning. 'Life does go on,' he thought while tucking a newspaper under his arm as he unlocked the door to his office. He was glad to be back at work even though he felt a little strange under the circumstances but decided that today would be a brand new start, a new beginning. He was determined to put the past two days behind him and move on to new and many successful days ahead. He had a publishing company to run and that is precisely what he planned to do.

After catching up on several telephone calls and sending email to a few clients, Gordon unfolded the morning newspaper and began to read the latest stock reports when all of a sudden he remembered HER manuscript. He had forgotten completely about it over the weekend and only now did he vaguely recall shoving it into the bottom drawer of his desk with the intention of reading it later. His pulse quickened with the thought of finding out more about the young woman whose death on the elevator constantly haunted him. He could feel the sweat dripping down the back of his neck as he opened his bottom desk drawer and removed the wrinkled, manilla envelope still covered with water spots and dirty smudges.

Gordon carefully unhooked the metal clasp and pulled out the neatly typed white pages onto his desk. Glancing down at the title page he felt his heart miss a beat and paused as he read: "Reflections In A Mirror" by Valerie Ficarro. His mind froze like an icicle in winter as he stared endlessly at the title and especially at the name of the author. He knew immediately her name was NOT one of the names listed in the newspaper, which meant that the woman who came to see him, the woman whose manuscript was laying in front of him, was still alive. Gordon breathed a huge sigh of relief as he would no longer have to endure the turmoil of feeling responsible for her death. Apparently she had taken the stairway on that fateful morning, just as he had always hoped.

Leaning back in his desk chair, he closed his eyes and wondered who exactly was this Valerie, what was her vocation, and would she ever try to get her book published with his company again. He was determined to find her and personally ask her these questions himself and more importantly find out about the title of her manuscript... the same title of the song that his daughter Jill had written. This seemed like a strange and mysterious coincidence to him and he would definitely ask Jill about it later that evening. Meanwhile he would focus all of his energy on how he was going to locate Valerie Ficarro, a woman whom he knew very little about. Gordon was not exactly sure where or how to begin his search but begin he would.

- 8 -

Everyone who knew Valerie Ficarro would agree that the one constant trait about her was her persistence. Whether she acquired this trait because she was a Scorpio or whether she had inherited it from her parents really did not matter. What mattered was that whenever she started a project, she would not stop until she got what she wanted, and the one thing in life, the only thing in life that she wanted, was to have her book published. This had been her biggest dream for as long as she could remember. When she was a little girl growing up in Fairport, a small town in upstate New York, she would always be seen with a notebook and a pencil in her hand ready to scribble down any thoughts, emotions, and ideas gained from her life experiences. Valerie wasn't interested in becoming a famous author, she simply considered herself a writer who loved to write.

It had taken her a little over two years to finish writing her first book which gave her a sense of accomplishment considering not only the financial cost involved but also the emotional cost as well. She never realized it would be a Herculean task to find a publisher who would be willing to publish it for her. After being turned down by several smaller companies, she decided to take an enormous risk and submit her manuscript to one of the largest and well-known publishers in Boston, the C & J Publishing Company. She had heard several rumors that the owner, Gordon Richardson, was a tyrant who would throw you out of his office in a lightning split second for something ridiculous, such as parting your hair on the wrong side. This image had caused Valerie to smile and it gave her the extra motivation and confidence needed to at least try to arrange a meeting with a publisher who had such an impatient reputation. And Valerie did try, even though friends had suggested that she was living in the Land of Oz and just wasting her precious time. At first she did not want to believe them, but after almost three years of continually trying to set up a meeting with Mr.Richardson and still no hope in sight, she was beginning to think that they were right.

Her persistence began to weaken as the months turned into years and many times Valerie was tempted to forget about her dream and pursue something different. One day she shared her frustration with Lily, an older woman with whom she worked, who was known throughout the office for her wisdom and intuition. Lily advised her to continue trying for at least one more year before giving up completely. If, at the end of one year, she still could not get in to see Mr. Richardson or any other publisher, then perhaps she should consider traveling instead of writing.

Valerie thought Lily's advice was sensible and just the right thing she needed to hear because one more year of rejection was about all she could emotionally handle. The word 'rejection' was never a word in her vocabulary, especially when it pertained to literary accomplishments. During her school years, her stories, essays, and poems were always the ones teachers selected to be either read, published, or at least acknowledged. Rejection was something that happened to other people, either to her classmates or friends, but never to her. She had majored in journalism while in college and upon graduation accepted a part-time job as a journalist with the local newspaper, 'The Daily Journal.' Working part-time was perfect for Val as it provided her with the necessary time needed to pursue her lifelong dream of writing a book. At the time, she lived with her elderly father who had always encouraged her to follow her heart. Unfortunately he passed away just two months before her book was completed, which was the reason why she dedicated it to him and was even more determined than ever to get it published in his honor.

The "one more year" attempt suggested by Lily was almost over the day Valerie miraculously was able to get an appointment with Gordon Richardson of the C & J Publishing Company. She felt just like a golfer hitting a hole-in-one, but somehow was able to restrain herself from shrieking joyfully into the ear of the secretary who called to inform her that Mr. Richardson would be happy to meet with her on Friday. Valerie immediately went shopping for a new outfit, which she was wearing that stormy day when she crossed the puddled street to his office. She always would wonder if it was because she looked so disheveled that Gordon Richardson did not spend very much time talking with her that rainy morning. Or maybe her hair was parted on the wrong side. She would never know for sure the exact reason because after leaving his office, she decided to take Lily's advice and give up writing and travel the world. Valerie took the stairway leading to the street below on that inauspicious day so that no one on the elevator would notice the tears streaming down her face. Once outside, her tears blended with the rain.

- 9 -

The first day back to work after the weekend was always the busiest day for Gordon Richardson and usually this presented no problem for him because, on any ordinary day he reveled in the constant hum of activity throughout the office, but this was no ordinary day. His duties as a publisher would have to be put on hold while he devoted the entire day to playing detective. He already had instructed Yvonne, his secretary, to call every Ficarro listed in the telephone book and if a Valerie Ficarro was located, he was to be notified immediately. Meanwhile, he would check out every possible connection to that name on the computer.

It was late Monday afternoon when Yvonne buzzed him to say that she had called every Ficarro listed and no one knew or had even heard of a woman by that name. Gordon's search on the Internet also turned up no leads. He was not going to let his disappointment and frustration get the best of him and he vowed to continue searching until he found her or someone who knew her. The vociferous rumblings in his stomach reminded him that he had missed lunch, so he decided to finally call it a day. It was already 3:15 p.m.in the afternoon and Jill and Luke would be home from school by now. Gordon was anxious to question Jill about the title of the song she wrote and wondered if by chance his daughter might even possibly know this woman, Valerie Ficarro.

Luke was busy making his favorite peanut butter and jelly sandwich when he was startled by the sound of the kitchen door opening and even more startled that it was his father.

'He's probably coming home early to check up on me,' thought Luke. "Hey dad, what are you doing home so soon?" asked his son with a knowing smirk.

Gordon only mumbled, "I'm taking a late lunch and I might need to use the computer, so don't get online like you usually do." Then he quickly snapped, "Where's your sister?"

"Where else? Upstairs on the phone talking with one of her friends. Most likely Scott." replied Luke.

Grabbing up half of Luke's sandwich as he bolted past the table, Gordon marched into the hallway and yelled loudly to his daughter:

"Jill !! Come downstairs immediately. I need to ask you something and it's very important."

"Oh darn, I have to go, Scott," she lamented. "Call me back later, okay? I will probably be home the rest of the day."

Jill reluctantly hung up the phone and wondered what her father could possibly want to ask her that was so urgent. Usually he never even bothered to say anything to her, especially when he first came home from work, and what was he doing home from work at this time of the day anyway?

"What's up, Dad?" Jill asked as she skipped down the stairs.

Gordon, swallowing a bite of Luke's sandwich, promptly rattled off two or three questions as bits of peanut butter squirted from the corners of his mouth.

"Where did you get the title for that song you wrote? Did you make it up yourself or copy it from somewhere? Do you know a woman by the name of Valerie Ficarro?"

Jill just stood there staring at this man who claimed to be her father, but who was acting like a total stranger. This man was not like the father she knew who always spoke slowly, distinctly, and in complete control.

"Whoa, Dad! Chill before you have a heart attack," said Jill while crossing her arms up in front of him.

Gordon cleared his throat, inhaled deeply and carefully began again.

"Okay, first of all, where did you get the idea for the name, "Reflections In A Mirror" for the song you wrote?"

Jill was not exactly sure why her father was asking this question, especially now, and wondered if she was in some kind of trouble. Should she just say that she made it up and hope he believed her, or should she tell him the truth. She decided on the latter and said:

"It was Scott's idea. His mom works with a woman who wrote a book with that title. He thought it was quite clever and suggested I write a song with the same name. I did not see any harm in using it since I'm not going to get my song published or anything."

Mr. Richardson listened carefully to Jill's explanation but the only sentence he really heard was, "His mom works with a woman who wrote a book with that title." Gordon tried his best to remain calm as he meticulously asked his daughter the next question.

"Where exactly does Scott's mother work?"

"She works at one of the local newspapers as an editor or something, but I'm not sure which paper. Dad, you're not going to call her are you? She will tell that lady we stole her book title and me and Scott could get in big trouble."

Gordon looked at his daughter with a sparkle in his eye and grinned.

"No need to worry your pretty little head off about it. If she does find out, I'm sure she would be flattered, not upset. Now please, call Scott and find out his mother's name and the newspaper where she works. I'll be waiting right here in the kitchen." Jill was halfway up the stairs when she excitedly shouted over her shoulder, "I already know his mother's first name. It's Sarah."

- 10 -

After three attempts to call 'The Daily Journal,' Gordon eventually reached the switchboard and was put on hold while waiting to be transferred to the Personnel Department. The stress and frustration were draining his energy and stamina and he could feel his eyelids beginning to droop as he waited for someone to pick up the phone. The anticipation and overwhelming excitement of finally locating Valerie kept him from dozing while he waited.

"Personnel. How may I direct your call?" asked the voice on the other end. "Valerie Ficarro, please," responded Gordon in a business-like tone. After a short pause, the woman replied, "May I ask who's calling?"

"My name is Gordon. Gordon Richardson of the C & J Publishing Company."

"Thank you, Mr. Richardson, but Ms. Ficarro is no longer employed here. Is there someone else with whom you would like to speak?"

Gordon was not prepared to hear that answer and instantly had to gather his composure and think expeditiously before hanging up. "Ummm...yes...can I speak with Sarah...Sarah Applegate."

"Just a minute, please and I will page her for you," said the switchboard operator very politely.

Sarah Applegate had been employed by 'The Daily Journal' for almost 22 years and the only time she missed work was when her son, Scott, was born. She had applied herself diligently throughout the years and was recently promoted to the position of Assistant Editor. Her responsibilities included hiring college graduates to work on a part-time basis in the Editorial Department, where she was respected and well-liked by all her colleagues.

"Hello, Mr. Richardson. It's so nice to hear from you," said Sarah picking up the phone. "I hope everything is okay with Scott and Jill. She's such a lovely girl."

"Hi Sarah," Gordon replied. "Yeah, she takes after her mother. Scott's a nice kid too, and they make a charming couple, but actually I'm calling about a different matter. A woman named Valerie who used to work in your department wrote a book entitled "Reflections In A Mirror," and it's very important that I get in touch with her. I was wondering if you knew how I can reach her."

"Oh....you must mean Valerie Ficarro. Yes, I was the one who hired her right after she graduated from college. She was an excellent journalist and very dedicated to her career so it certainly was a complete surprise when she quit so suddenly last week. I have tried calling her house but the phone number has been disconnected and I've heard rumors through the grapevine that she will be moving to a small town in Italy to work at her brother's restaurant.

"Oh, I see." replied Gordon in a softer tone. "Do you happen to have her home address? he asked enthusiastically. "Perhaps it might be possible for me to catch her before she leaves for Italy."

- 11 -

It was shortly after eight the next morning when Gordon telephoned his secretary to tell her to cancel all of his appointments for the next few days as he would not be coming into the office for a while.

"I hope you are feeling okay, Mr. Richardson," she expressed with concern.

"Yes. I'm fine Yvonne. I just need to take a few days off to clear up a few personal matters. If something urgent arises, you can try to reach me at home or on my cell.

Hanging up the phone, Gordon glanced down at the crumbled piece of yellow paper on which he had scribbled Valerie's address. He was not familiar with the street, Sheldon Avenue, but Sarah had told him she thought it was near the Patrick Henry Public Library located on the other side of town, about a half hour away. Gulping down the last drop of his cold coffee and snatching up his car keys from the counter, he quietly shut the kitchen door behind him as he left the house.

Gordon spent the half hour drive across town thinking exclusively about what he was going to say to Valerie and wondering what his next step would be if she had already left for Europe. He had only met her that day when she came into his office to drop off her manuscript but he remembered her deep dimpled smile and that she was very attractive. He frowned as he recalled how abrupt he was with her and that he had dismissed her almost instantly.

Gordon chuckled to himself as he realized that he still had not yet read her manuscript and told himself that he would definitely read it when he returned to his office. He had just pulled up at a traffic light and was waiting for it to turn green, when he spotted the Patrick Henry Public Library across the street. Valerie's house had to be close by.

Gordon noticed that the faded yellow, two-story frame house desperately needed to be painted, as he parked his car in front of 116 Sheldon Avenue. He was extra-cautious as he slowly walked up the dilapidated porch steps which were strewn with wet newspapers. The appearance of Valerie's house, along with the closed curtains, indicated that no one was currently at home but, nevertheless, he opened the torn screen door and knocked loudly. He waited for a reasonable length of time for someone to answer, but when no one did, he went around the house to try the back door. Disappointment and discouragement were written on his face, but he had come this far to find her and he was not going to give up so easily.

What Gordon Richardson did not foresee was just how far he would have to go and how enormously difficult it was going to be to find Valerie, a woman who was beginning to dominate his every thought.

- 12 -

The tears that were streaming down Valerie's somber face as she left Mr. Richardson's office had turned to uncontrollable sobs by the time she reached the bottom of the stairs. She had invested so much time and energy into the writing of her book that this final rejection was more than she could handle. She sat in her car for a long while before regaining enough composure and control to drive home safely. Lily was right, she thought. I should give up writing and try something different. On her way home, Val called 'The Daily Journal' and told them she was very sorry, but she would no longer be working for them. She apologized for giving such a short notice but due to personal reasons, she would be leaving Boston and moving to Italy to live with her brother.

She waited until she got home before placing her next call to the Quick-Flight Travel Agency to arrange a trip to Europe within the next day or two. There was no longer any reason for her to remain in Boston, and the thought of seeing her brother again brought a tiny smile to her tear-stained face.

When her father died she missed him terribly, but it was his constant support and positive encouragement of her writing that she missed the most. If it were not for him she would never have finished her book and even though it seemed unlikely to ever get published, she would always have "Reflections

In A Mirror" to remind her of how fortunate she was to have had such a wonderful father.

Her parents had gotten divorced when she was still a little girl growing up in Fairport and Valerie was raised by her dad, while her older brother, Vince, went to live with their mother. She considered herself to be the lucky one, as she adored her father who always showered her with his love and affection. Materially, he was only able to afford the basic necessities for his little girl due to the fact that he would spend most of his paycheck in the local bars drinking and arguing politics with his cronies.

Although she and Vince never saw much of each other while growing up, they did manage to stay in touch and after their father passed away, Vince begged his sister to move to Italy with him. When he was young he loved to cook and would spend hours in the kitchen creating a variety of Italian dishes while driving his Mama crazy with thousands of questions. She was the one who suggested that he get an education at a culinary school in New York City and perhaps one day he might be able to open up his own restaurant. Vince pursued his dream and was now the owner and head chef at one of Taranto's finest dining establishments. He had often asked his sister to move to Italy and join him in his restaurant business, but Valerie was busy pursuing her own dream. Vince made her promise that some day in the future she would make the trip to Italy and have dinner with him in his restaurant, The Sono Qui.

The constant ringing of the telephone brought Valerie back in the moment but she hesitated before answering it. She knew it was the travel agency calling about her flight arrangements making her ambiguous decision final. She gathered up her courage and walked slowly towards the phone, thinking that now would be the perfect time for her long, over-due visit with Vince. Her voice was a mixture of exhilaration and trepidation as she picked up the receiver and softly whispered:

"Hello"

- 13 -

Valerie was just beginning to doze off when the pilot's voice over the plane's intercom aroused her fully awake. She listened as he announced:

"We are approaching Taranto International Airport and will be landing within the next twenty minutes. Please fasten your seat belts and remain seated until the plane has come to a complete stop. It has been our pleasure to serve you. Thank you for flying Air Italia.

It had been a long flight and she was yearning to stretch her legs which by now were very stiff and a little swollen. She had never been to Italy before but Vince had assured her that she would fall in love with the country and its people, and would enjoy living such a beautiful lifestyle that she would never have to worry about getting homesick. She was not completely convinced by his enthusiastic comments, but was determined to give it a serious try knowing that she could always return to the United States whenever she wanted.

Valerie planned to live with her brother while working at his restaurant until she was able to save up enough money to rent a villa by herself. Learning to speak the Italian language was one of her big concerns, but Vince had given her his word of honor that it was a fairly easy language to learn and if he could learn it, she certainly would have no problem.

She felt the bump as the wheels of the airplane touched down and looking out the window she intuitively sensed that living in Italy was going to be an exciting adventure, one that she would hopefully enjoy and treasure.

- 14 -

"Buona Sera, Signorina Ficarro," exclaimed Giuseppe as Valerie walked toward the table to take his order. She knew it was Friday without even looking at the calendar. Joe came in for lunch every Friday and would always order the same thing: a tossed salad with endive, two slices of pizza with anchovies, and a glass of red wine.

Valerie smiled, "Ciao Joe, the usual?" "Si, an a maybe this a time with a little a kiss for dessert?" he winked.

The Italian men loved to flirt with the single girls, especially single girls from America! Valerie liked Joe because he was charming and harmless but some of the other men who frequented her brother's restaurant sometimes caused her a few problems. She was able to handle most of them after working at the The Sono Qui for almost six years, but there were still occasions when she would have to depend on Vince to rescue her.

Living with her brother when she first arrived in Italy was a blessing, but now that Valerie had a villa of her own, she was able to travel and explore the beautiful countryside which helped her to forget, if only momentarily, her life back in the U.S.

Once in a while, something would remind her of Lily, the woman at the newspaper office where she had once worked. Lily had been a lifesaver for

Valerie giving her good advice and direction and suggesting perhaps she may now want to experience traveling and put writing aside temporarily. She was probably retired from the newspaper business by now and spending her leisurely days traveling too.

Valerie often thought about her other friends at 'The Daily Journal' with whom she had worked and wondered what changes had occurred in their lives. Were they still meeting for drinks after work on Fridays to gossip and giggle about certain men in their office and to share with each other their plans for the weekend. Reminiscing about her life in Boston would always lead her back to the time in her life when she was consumed by her passion for writing and would spend days buried in words and thoughts while working on her book. Ah, yes, her book. That was one of the reasons she had left the states six years ago. Sometimes she would allow herself to play with the idea of having her book translated into the Italian language with the possibility of getting it published in Italy. She laughed at the thought of thumbing her nose at the C & J Publishing Company, especially at the president. She could not recall his name but she would never forget the way he patronized her that day in his office when she dropped off her manuscript.

Valerie's eyes would fill and often brim over with tears whenever she reflected on those days which now seemed like a lifetime ago. Occasionally she would yearn to unpack her manuscript and read it, but she never did. Maybe some day she would blow the dust off from it and give it to her brother, Vince, to read, In the meantime, she would just keep busy with her life in Italy and leave her days as a writer in the past.

- 15 -

Claire was beginning to feel that she had skimmed through every bridal magazine that was ever published and was still not able to find a mother-of-the bride dress that she liked. It was either the wrong style or the wrong color. She was seriously considering asking one of her friends to design and sew the perfect dress for her, but there was not enough time as there were so many other responsibilities she needed to handle in order to prepare for her daughter's upcoming wedding.

She had known for a long time that Jill and Scott, who had been dating steadily for several years, would eventually get married. She just thought it would be better if they waited until after finishing college before beginning their life together as man and wife. Several times during the past year she had asked Gordon to advise them to wait until after graduation, but he had gladly given his approval. He did not see any problem if they wanted to get married while still attending college. Gordon and Claire usually never agreed on anything and after almost 23 years of marriage that was not about to change.

When it came to his daughter, Gordon Richardson could never say no. Jill had him wrapped tightly around her finger and the strings around his heart were even tighter. He felt blessed that she had found someone who would be able to provide her not only with material possessions but also with the warmth, comfort, and security she definitely deserved. Scott came from a well-respected family whose father, Tom Applegate, was the Town Attorney and his mother, Sarah, worked at the local newspaper. They had always treated Jill as if she were their own daughter. Gordon would always be grateful for Mr. Applegate's sincere concern and support when Luke and his friends were caught robbing a liquor store. The judge had ruled it a first-class felony and ordered him to serve two years in jail, but Mr. Applegate managed to get his sentence reduced to one year with good behavior. Although Luke was released from prison only three months ago, Scott nevertheless had asked him to be an usher in his wedding party.

Thinking about the past was never easy for Claire as it had been a long journey with many ups and downs, and if she remembered correctly, it was mostly downs when it involved Luke. He had always been the black sheep of the family and had given them a a lot of headaches growing up, which in hindsight were trivial when compared with the heartache he caused them later in life. Claire would often speculate how Luke may never have gotten into so much trouble if she and Gordon had been better parents and more involved in his life. In her heart she would always blame herself because of the lifestyle she lived during his formative years... a selfish lifestyle centered on her own needs and desires.

Claire preferred not to think about the years when Luke was growing up because doing so served no purpose and only filled her with rage and anger, directed mainly at herself for being such a fool. She had naively believed the man with whom she was having an affair was as deeply in love with her as she was with him. When her children were raised, and living on their own, she had planned to divorce Gordon and marry him. At the time it all seemed so simple and uncomplicated. She and Evan had been a twosome for years and they had often discussed and planned their future together as man and wife. Which is why Claire was totally and utterly disoriented the day Evan told her he was leaving her for someone else. and the hardest part for her to accept was that he had become involved with a man ten years younger than himself. To think that she had sacrificed time with her family and friends for this, this mess. It kept her in tears for months.

"Hey mom," said Jill interrupting her mother's thoughts as she bounced into the kitchen. I only had one class at school today so I thought I'd drive over and see if you had any luck picking out your dress for my wedding?"
"No, I haven't been able to find one yet that I really like, but don't worry, I am determined to get it by the end of the week. Has Margaret finally finished hemming your gown?" Claire asked nervously.

"No, but she did ask me to stop in on Friday for a fitting so I'm hoping I will be able to bring it home soon. I want to make sure Dad does not see it, so if he happens to come home from work early, I'll have to sneak it in somehow. He will never understand why he has to wait until my wedding day to see it, when he is the one paying for it."

Claire smiled at her daughter's giddiness and replied: "Well, it's a good thing you're getting married before your Dad retires. Luckily he has enough money reserved to pay for the cost of a lavish wedding, or else you and Scott might have had to elope.

"Oh fiddle-ly-dee" laughed Jill, trying to sound like Scarlet O'Hara. "Mom, you know Dad would even borrow the money if necessary in order to pay for my wedding."

Claire silently nodded in agreement.

- 16

The sun was setting as Gordon leaned over his desk to switch on the light in his office, which was growing darker with each passing minute. Looking at his watch he was surprised to see it was way past six o'clock, his usual quitting time.

'Nothing was usual anymore,' he thought, especially during these past months while he was busy preparing himself, not only for Jill's upcoming wedding, but also for his departure from the C & J publishing company.

He was only 46 years old, but after giving it much thought and consideration, he had decided to let the younger people run his company as he stepped aside. The idea of selling out had occurred to him, but he was not able to take that final step. This had been his life for years and to give it up completely was out of the question. It was a competitive business, which he thrived on in his younger days, but as he grew older it was becoming a burden that was sapping his energy. He now wanted to spend that energy indulging in days of quiet leisure and relaxation, two luxuries he never allowed himself to experience and enjoy. He had the penetrating impression that the story of his life was about to end and a new chapter was about to begin.

Gordon had almost finished emptying out the drawers of his desk when his eyes fell on HER manuscript. A tiny smile crept across his lips as he vaguely recalled those days........days that now seemed to have happened in another lifetime. He flipped through the pages of her book while his mind flipped through the years, and he could not help but wonder what ever happened to that woman named Valerie. He felt sorry that he was never able to get in touch with her and even sorrier that he never took the time to read her book.

'Well, I certainly will have the time now,' thought Gordon, as he carefully placed it into the box of papers he was taking home.

- 17 -

St. Peter's Church had never before looked so beautiful to Gordon. The alter, sprinkled with bunches of lavender, was adorned with an assortment of tulips and white carnations that were not only picturesque to the eye but also permeated the entire church with a fragrance beyond description.

He felt Jill's hand lightly squeeze his arm as the organist started to play, "Reflections In A Mirror," the song that she and Scott had chosen for their wedding ceremony. He smiled at his gorgeous daughter who looked absolutely stunning and gave her a wink as they began their procession down the aisle.

Claire was already sitting in the front pew wearing the silk, beige two-piece dress that she finally had chosen for this day. The long jacket was perfect as it concealed the tightness of the skirt across her slightly pudgy hips. She had planned to lose a few pounds before Jill's wedding, but obviously should have known better. She was very familiar with plans that never work out.

Her thoughts drifted back to her own wedding day when she and Gordon were so very young and crazy in love, just like Scott and Jill were today. 'Why did those days have to change,' she pondered even though she knew deep down that all of life changes....nothing stays the same. She thought about

Evan and could not help but wonder whatever happened to him and if he and his friend were still together.

Claire knew that it was only a matter of time before Gordon would file for divorce and they would each go their separate ways. She had no definite plans for the future but felt secure knowing she would be able to cope with whatever life had in store for her. Now that Jill was getting married and Luke was planning to join the Army, she would enjoy being independent and free from her motherly responsibilities. Of course, she would always worry about her children, but they were adults now and it was time to let them play out their own lives.

She watched with affection as Gordon carefully lifted the lace veil from their daughter's face and tenderly place a kiss on Jill's cheek before joining her in the front pew.

- 18 -

Jill and Scott were still on their honeymoon in Florida the day Gordon sat down on the living room sofa to open the large cardboard box from his office. It had been stored up in the attic for six years and he had completely forgotten all about it until Claire happened to mention it to him the day she was leaving.

"Gordon, I have finished packing up the things from the attic that I want to take with me but there is a box with your books and papers from the office still up there. Don't you think it's about time to get rid of it?" asked Claire while carrying suitcases out to her car.

"Maybe I will one of these days," he replied nonchalantly. Gordon was not going to let Claire have the satisfaction of knowing that he did not even remember storing it up there. He stood at the door and watched as Claire drove away then turned and immediately headed upstairs to the attic. He had mixed emotions as he began to sort through the box containing bittersweet memories of the days when he was president of his own publishing company. He laughed out loud when he read a few of the frivolous notes he had written to his secretary, Yvonne. He had always appreciated her dedication and loyalty throughout the years and was amazed that she was able to endure his strict rules and sarcastic manner for such a long time.

'I paid her a fantastic salary and gave her prodigious raises every year, which may have been one reason,' he thought to himself. He felt slightly remorseful that he had never bothered to inquire about her after he left the company and wondered if she was still working or was now enjoying days of leisure which she definitely deserved.

Gordon spent the next hour or two reading and sorting out the other papers and memorabilia and had almost emptied the entire box when his eyes fell on HER manuscript. It was still very winkled and dirty and the pages had turned slightly yellow but if he squinted, he was able to make out the title, "Reflections In A Mirror" by Valerie Ficarro. He felt like the earth was spinning in reverse as a stream of memories began to flood his consciousness.

Leaning back in the chair, Gordon shut his eyes and pictured her as she entered his office that wet morning. He could remember every physical detail about her from her sparkling blue eyes and dimpled smile right down to her curvy hips and sexy legs. He had known subconsciously that he had been very attracted to her that day. Unfortunately it was a very unsettling time in his life and he vaguely remembered how rude and uncivil he was to her and how he simply had shoved her manuscript into his desk drawer and had forgotten all about it. Until now.

His thoughts jumped ahead to the time when he spent days searching for her, even driving out to her house in a small town in upstate N.Y. He was anxious to find her and ask her about the title of her manuscript, the very manuscript that he now held in his hands. After all these years, he was finally going to read it.

- 19 -

Valerie's story begins when a young woman named Michele Ruggerio, is desperately trying to find a publisher for a novel that she has written. After many unsuccessful attempts, she gets an appointment with David Smithfield, who is the president of one of the largest publishing companies in New York City.

'It seems like Valerie is writing her own autobiography,' Gordon thought to himself after reading the first couple of pages. He had no idea of how accurate his observation was, nor the shocking revelation that was yet to be revealed.

In her book, David Smithfield is an arrogant, self-centered person who spends most of his time at the office and very little time at home with his wife, Olivia, and their two children. He discovers that his wife is having an affair and his son, Steve, is attracted to trouble like a magnet. His musically-gifted daughter, Rosemarie, is the only family member close to his heart whom he loves unconditionally.

'Christ,' thought Gordon, while rubbing his eyes in disbelief. First she was writing about herself in the character of Michele, and now this David character is exactly like ME. She doesn't know me how could she possibly know all about me?' The story becomes even more mysterious as he reads that David is an exact carbon copy of himself, possessing the same personality, the same emotions, and sharing the same life experiences that he has had.

Gordon is fascinated by her character, David, who is a reflection of himself. This is a strange paradox and very puzzling to him. He impulsively flips the pages to the end of the book to find out how the story.... the story of his life will end.

In the last two chapters of Valerie's book, the main character, Michele, finally gives up the idea of having her manuscript published, quits her job at the newspaper office, and moves to Taranto, a small town in Italy, to live with her brother and work in his restaurant, The Sono Qui. David and Olivia get divorced after their daughter is married and their son who caused them a lot of heartache joins the Army. One day years later, David is searching through a box of papers from his attic and finds the manuscript that he had stuffed in his desk drawer the day Michele came to see him. He finally reads it and by the time he comes to the last page he knows what he must do.

Gordon is now lost in a a cloud of amazement and disbelief at what he is has just read. It all seems surreal to him. How could Valerie's book be so explicit in the description of his life, right down to every minute detail? Things like this just can't happen or can they? He is ready to explode with curiosity and can't wait until he finds out what her character David is now going to do.

Gordon sat in awe for a long, long time reflecting on what he had just read. Valerie's character, David, had revealed to him what he himself must now do. Early tomorrow morning he will make airline reservations for his trip to Taranto, Italy, find Valerie and return her manuscript to her.

- 20 -

The sun was shining brightly as Gordon hailed a taxi from the terminal. His plane had landed in Italy hours before, but due to a mix-up at the baggage claim, he had to wait more than two hours before finally getting his luggage.

"The Sono Qui Restorante," he told the taxi driver in an exhausted tone.

"Si, Signor," replied the driver. "It's about a 30 minute ride."

"That's fine," said Gordon, He had waited years for this moment that another thirty minutes did not concern him. What did concern him was her manuscript that he now gripped tightly in his hands and what Valerie's reaction would be when she saw him. Would she even remember who he was and how rudely he had treated her that day in his office so many years ago.

It seemed like an eternity to him before the taxicab finally pulled over to the curb and the driver pointed to the restaurant on the corner. "Over there is The Sono Qui Restorante, Signor." "Molto Grazie," answered Gordon.

He could hear his heart thumping loudly as he stood for a moment outside of the restaurant collecting his thoughts while watching young Italian children playing hopscotch on the sidewalk. He was grateful for the brief distraction which gave him time to think about Valerie and how their roles were now reversed like reflections in a mirror. He was entering her restaurant just as years ago she had entered his office. Taking a few deep breaths, he quietly opened the door and stepped inside.

The restaurant was filled with people eating, drinking, and engrossed in low-tone conversations and as Gordon patiently waited, he noticed the artistic decorations throughout the main dining area. The tables were adorned with flowers of brilliant colors and the walls were covered with huge flags from every country. The American Flag, hanging in the center, was the largest one and he felt a warm sense of pride standing in front of it. In a few minutes a waitress approaches him and asks if he would prefer a booth or a table.

"Ummm...act...actually.... I have come to...to... meet someone," stuttered Gordon. He immediately remembered how Valerie had stuttered when she came into his office, and again, like a reflection in a mirror, he was doing exactly the same thing.

"Does a woman by the name of Valerie Ficarro work here?" he finally managed to ask without stuttering.

"Si. Un momento. She is in the kitchen and I will check to see if she is available to speak with you. "Wait here," per favore," the waitress replied using a mixture of Italian and English.

About fifteen minutes later, Gordon watches as an attractive, dark-haired woman wearing an enormous, deep-dimpled smile walks towards him. He could feel his legs beginning to weaken and the palms of his hands starting to sweat as Valerie approaches. He is acutely aware of the tight lump in his throat making him feel like a teenager and the emotions stirring from within almost bring tears to his eyes as Valerie stops directly in front of him. Gordon hesitates for a second while clearing his throat and with slight trepidation reaches out, hands her the manuscript, and says: "Hi. I'm David."

Gazing deeply into his sparkling eyes, Valerie nods.

"Hi. I'm Michele."

As Valerie slips into Gordon's outstretched arms, she whispers in his ear:

"I have been expecting you. What took you so long?"

THE END